Wait For Me

SUZANNE JOY FABER

illustrated by

LIVI GOSLING

AMP&RSAND, INC.

Chicago • New Orleans

"Wait for me!" Henry called
to his brother. "Wait for me!"

But his brother did not wait.
He was bigger than Henry
and walking with his friends.

"Wait for me!"
called Henry.

"Wait for me!" Now he was almost as big and soon would be able to keep up.

"Wait for me!"

Daisy called to her brother Henry. "Wait for me!"

And Henry did
wait for Daisy

because he remembered
what it felt like to be small

and because he was nice.

ISBN 978-0996252522

Design: David Robson, Robson Design

Published by
AMPERSAND, INC.
1050 North State Street
Chicago, Illinois 60610

———

203 Finland Place
New Orleans, Louisiana 70131

www.ampersandworks.com

Published and produced in the U.S.A.
Printed in Canada

For Rick